IN THE BOOK I'M READING

STORIES

ONE BIRD BOOKS
Available at amazon.com
and barnesandnoble.com

Door by Mary Kane

The Ant and the Map by Judith Benét Richardson

Harlequin's Guitar: A Fable in 67 Improvisations
by Jim Morgan

Little Hours: A Novel by Lil Copan

Procession of Souls by Jim Morgan

Luminous: a forty-four day exchange while wandering
The Tibetan Book of the Dead, poems and art
by Mary Kane and Mark Bilokur

Black Apple: Collected Prose Poems 1975 to 2022
by Eric H. Edwards

IN THE BOOK I'M READING

STORIES

MARY KANE

One Bird Books, Hatchville, Mass.

Acknowledgements

FRiGG   "Not Nude, Not Descending a
         Staircase, No. 2"
         "Writing Class"
         "The Coat"
         "The Reasons"
         "Lamp"
         "The Problem"
MoonPark Review "Thank You Letter"
Smokelong Quarterly "Practice"

Editor: Jim Morgan

Design and layout: Jim Morgan
Cover design: Mary Kane and Jim Morgan
Cover art by Mark Bilokur

ISBN: 978-1-7339200-6-3

One Bird Books
35 Brush Hill Road
Hatchville, MA 02536
www.onebirdbooks.com
onebirdbooks@gmail.com

Contents

PRACTICE

I met my husband on the path that runs along the marsh in our town. He pretended he was my ex-husband. It's a habit of his. Actually, we'd woken early that day, sipped coffee from twin mugs, read quietly side by side for about 45 minutes, then gotten up and dressed in long johns and turtlenecks, readying ourselves for our ritual winter morning walk. We were about two miles into the walk when he pretended to run into me on the path. He's practicing, he says, so that, in the unlikely event that in some distant future we happen to split up, if we then run into each other in a public place, we'll know how to behave.

"Hi," he says, motioning to the person not standing beside me, the person I've apparently left him for, and stretches out his hand as though to introduce himself. No response. Whomever I'm with is either very unfriendly or doesn't recognize my ex-husband and is surprised at this man in the fur-lined coat and tasseled hat stopping us on the path, no other humans in sight in any direction, the gray February morning light so pallid it seems the day might collapse.

My husband as ex-husband turns his torso ever so slightly to the right, in order to address me rather than my mute partner. He looks down very briefly at his shoes, and because he looks there I can't help but follow with my eyes. I think about how my husband sometimes suffers from soreness of the toe. Maybe these shoes I've just glanced at, following his gaze, are the reason for that soreness. They look rather worn. He seems so fragile all of a sudden, there on the path, alone, his toe quite possibly sore, in his new unmarried life. "How's Tolstoy going?" I ask. "Did Prince Andrei get wounded yet?" I'm tempted to invite him to dinner, if my partner wouldn't mind. Or maybe ask him to coffee, just the two of us.

And then I remember the fifteen years of loneliness I discovered in my hips only yesterday. When I look again at my husband, he's kneeling down on the path, scratching the invisible head of his invisible dog, behind the ears, vigorously.

"Come on, Rex," he says, "we'd better get going."

Not Nude, Not Descending a Staircase, No. 2

Last night in the middle of the night I awoke from a disturbing dream, thirsty, and, deciding to go downstairs to get a glass of water, I rolled onto my side, climbed out of bed, and approached the staircase, intending to descend to the kitchen, but when I reached the head of the stairs, I could see, silhouetted by the moonlight, for there was a nearly full moon last night, the form of the cat at the foot of the stairs, crouched in front of the screen door. Or behind the screen door depending how you look at it. It was night. The cat is black and white but looked all black in that light.

The cat was inside the house at the foot of the stairs at the screen door where he often likes to sit and watch the world outside. In our family we sometimes find it funny that the cat so often sits in front of a screen because we live in such a screen-obsessed culture, but the screen the cat sits before is the kind that lets air through and keeps out flies and other insects, the kind therefore that one looks through not at. The cat does not, as far as

I know, ever look at a screen since we are not TV watchers and the cat hasn't a smart phone, though if there happens to be a moth or fly on the screen, then that might be another story.

I wanted to go down in the night for a glass of water, but the cat, only nine months old and still a kitten with kittenish energy, sometimes gets very feisty at night and I was afraid he'd attack my feet or ankles if I descended the stairs. As I stood there, regarding the cat from my great height, I wasn't nude, since I generally wear a T-shirt to sleep even on fairly hot and humid nights, though I felt sort of fractured. I felt like I, or my consciousness, at any rate, was made of about 55 sharply angled pieces, and I had the distinct impression that they could quite easily shift so their edges no longer lined up into the normally more seamless version of me that most people who know me encounter on a regular basis. My feeling fractured, I realized, might have been the result of the combination of the moonlight and the ceiling fan since it is summer after all and fairly hot, which is why the door was open so all that moonlight was flooding into the living room and the staircase and we often keep the ceiling fan on to try to cool the house, and I began to wonder if the interaction of the moonlight with the ceiling fan was perhaps creating a subtle strobe effect that was altering my sense of myself, causing me to feel more and more unsettled.

So I stood there at the top of the stairs, not descending, so as to stop the parts of me, which were a bit like plates in a lesson on plate tectonics, from sliding and shifting and turning me into an even more fractured version of myself and also to prevent the cat's attacking my feet. And even though I wasn't nude and wasn't yet descending, I thought about Marcel Duchamp and the uproar his painting of the reimagined human form caused when it debuted, how it was roundly rejected by the *Salon des Indépendants'* hanging committee, and later, when it showed in New York, how it met with mockery and ridicule. I stood there, recalling how I'd read once that Duchamp's brothers wanted the artist to change the title of his at the time not-yet-famous work because, they insisted, a nude doesn't descend stairs, a nude reclines. What, I thought, if the reclining nude were upstairs in his/her house and happened to get thirsty and need to go to the kitchen for a glass of water?

But as I've said, I wasn't nude and so, I reasoned, my descent, even if I fragmented on the spot, was bound to be less scandalous than its artistic predecessor. Still, as I stood there at the top of the stairs, disorientation mounting, it also occurred to me that were I, meaning all 55 shards of me, to shift the way I imagined I/they might, such a shift would most likely happen rather quickly, and that might cause the cat to go really nuts. So I stepped backwards, very slowly and quietly, one bare foot at a time, until I was back in my bedroom where I climbed back into bed and told myself I wasn't all that thirsty anyway.

A Little Tent

I was reading in bed and snow was falling outside when the woman in my book said she was reading in bed when in her book a woman walked by wearing a yellow headscarf. The woman in my book was reading a story by Albert Camus and she felt glad for the woman in the headscarf that she happened into a Camus story, her fate being greater than had she appeared in the story of a lesser writer, and I tend to identify with the narrators in the books I am reading, so I began to wonder at the weather outside of the bedroom of the woman in my book. In this part of her book, it turns out it is raining, which is the reason for the scarf over the passing woman's head, though not the reason for the color of the scarf. Here, outside my room, snow was falling, and though I couldn't coordinate all the weather, I began to think that maybe I was the woman in the book I was reading since the sentence that caught *her* attention in Camus' story also caught *my* attention in her story. Maybe we are like a ladder of readers and one can descend all the way to the woman in the headscarf. Maybe she had only one headscarf, which happened to be yellow, and maybe this was terrifically fortunate, since without it she wouldn't have caught Camus' eye, but I'm thinking he may not actually have seen anyone wearing a headscarf. Maybe Camus was sitting in his study, looking out the window, and the day was terrifically gray, inducing in him a longing for color. Out of this dull mid-winter longing, he may have invented the woman and her yellow scarf to save his mind's eye from the grays and browns and endlessly colorless afternoons of his mid-life. Maybe he looked at his lover and felt annoyed by the expression her back made as she folded linens and placed them silently in the drawer of a side table and knew he was in trouble since when our annoyance begins to be triggered by things as mute as our lover's back, we know that ennui and our inner critic have begun to conspire against us. Outside my window snow continued to fall so I became pretty certain that I was myself and not the narrator of the book I was reading, but when I tried to settle into my book again, my thoughts became unruly. They were like fans at a football game, drinking beer and waving fists in the air, shouting complaints at no one in particular, or they were like armed guards barging in on my bedroom, breaking the peacefulness of my reading in bed. I could no longer see the words on the page. Or I could see them but I couldn't find my way to them. Sometimes reading is like trying to swim to a far off destination through a choppy ocean, the distance very difficult to judge from the water. Plus, the current is strong and you swim very hard, exerting your whole body, but you seem to make little to no progress. Maybe you are even losing ground, being pulled against your destination by waves and tides. I decided to close my eyes and rest the book with its spine open on my chest. I like this position. The book makes a little tent. I don't push it open too hard. I don't want to harm its spine. I wonder how many people get buried like this, a slim volume of poetry or prose cracked open on their chest. Choosing the book could be difficult if you have a lot of books you love. I love the book that is open in a little tent on my chest. I picture going in there on a summer night, reading by flashlight while outside mosquitoes buzz, longing to get into my tent. Now I can go back to my book in the present with snow falling outside because the tent of my book has brought me through space and time to a state of relaxed concentration where the football fans and armed guards have wandered off to bother someone else and I can see that indeed, the scene has changed and now it is snowing in the pages of my book and snowing outside of my bedroom, and look, now the woman in my book is putting on her long wool coat and leaving her classroom in the middle of teaching her class. She says nothing to the students because she is leaving to meet her lover and the students don't need to know that. She writes a sentence on the board which says, "Continue to read quietly until the end of class" and walks out the door, passing underneath the round face of the school clock on her way out, certain that the students will do what the words on the board tell them to do.

FAILURE

If you wonder what these two women are doing, standing on a path at night in winter moonlight, looking up, taking a step or two in one direction, looking up again and sharing a few words with each other before moving a few feet in another direction, repeating their motions, I will tell you. They are trying to count wild turkeys roosting in treetops. The turkeys, backlit by the moon, appear as fat black silhouettes, like the fantastic black petals of enormous flowers. The women are mainly unsuccessful in obtaining an accurate count. One moment one will count 30, and the other 28. A moment later, one will count 29 and the other 31. Neither is convinced of the accuracy of any of the numbers. In this they nonetheless delight.

Well Into It

Well into our marriage I learn that before we met, you were a champion bowler.

New Old Couple

Last night, my husband and I were in bed. As is fairly customary, he was lying down talking to no one in particular, and I was propped up against my pillows, reading. After a short time, I put down my book and was adjusting my pillows for sleep before turning out the bedside lamp when my husband looked at me and said that wow, when I turned whatever way I had just turned, I looked exactly like Jack, my father. At that moment, in response to his statement, I looked at him. And he looked exactly like Norman, his father. Then I turned off the light. And there we lay, side by side, two old men holding hands in the dark.

Writing Class

My aunt Arlene likes to stand in the kitchen, at the counter, cracking eggs into a mixing bowl. If I ask her what she's up to, she says she's writing. I believe her though it's hard to say or see exactly how that works, mechanically speaking. One day recently, she said I probably wanted to know what eggs had to do with writing, and though I didn't really require an explanation, since I trust her, she told me anyway. She said she likes to read a lot and that every writer she reads gets compressed like a language egg in the ear inside her mind, and when she wants to write, she has to crack all the eggs and mix them together so that her words, the ones forming in her mind, won't get drowned out by any one writer's compressed presence. I pointed out that the eggs she was cracking weren't made of language and weren't in her head, and she said she was aware of that but it did the trick, and whatever did the trick is her motto. But then, because she doesn't like to waste, she ends up making a lot of omelets, and she then has to find people to feed the omelets to, which she does by walking door to door in the neighborhood and delivering omelets to anyone who wants one. That makes for a good feeling of neighborliness in the neighborhood and is also sort of time consuming, and I said I thought it probably detracts from her writing but she said no, she is writing then too, all the egg activities are part of the writing, even cleaning the plates when the neighbors return them, for she always delivers the omelets on china plates because if you have good dishes, why not use them. I said it was interesting the way a person could be writing all the time without anyone knowing it, and she said that was true and too many people live under the misconception that to be writing means you are sitting at a desk or with a laptop on your lap or are somewhere you can't identify, in bed, dying, your fingers wrapped around a pencil that is getting smaller and smaller, with another one you misplaced in your bed somewhere, and an old notebook, while men in greatcoats and uncomfortable hats knock on your skull from the inside trying to get written into your story, but she was thinking of teaching a writing class that would involve a lot of reading aloud and omelet preparation and dish washing and definitely lots of walks. Then, at the end of the course, the writers could all get together, and each one would read his or her story aloud while the others in the group lay on benches wrapped up in parkas and watched winter clouds scud across blue sky if the day were windy enough, or they might even nap, allowing each story to waft in through their sleeping ears gently like *lake water lapping with low sounds by* some shore someplace, and then she said that's exactly what she was talking about with the eggs, that last little bit, a bit of compressed language egg that hadn't blended completely enough, and did I think people would like to take the class.

That Thing

The wife had that thing, for a minute, or not even a minute, and the husband made peanut sauce. And yes, her libido fell into a torpor. But she had hope and a blue tarp and a few bungee cords, which had to be useful. An eagle'd been spotted. A storm promised to obliterate the weekend. The cat slept well and cleaned himself expertly.

The wife had that thing she had found in a book. And then the air ate it, or the fire. She had it when she encountered the word *velleity* in the book about a man with a stiff leg and then two stiff legs who knocked on his mother's skull to communicate, when he could find her. Years ago, before the cellphone, the wife had had a neighbor, downstairs, who had astrally projected the blue light of himself upstairs to walk across her kitchen to check on her.

And it was true that the wife's mother had never liked her. It only came out in pronouncements regarding characters in TV shows. She was another thing, her mother, a mouthpiece for patriarchy and consumer culture. Some people were. Streaming widely held beliefs during lulls in the action. The mother didn't know the meaning of the word *misogyny*, as if a poor vocabulary excused one's perspective.

But the thing. The wife saw it as a prized, dark, seed-sized capsule. She dug it out from paragraphs where a girl had died and then didn't die. She found it in a dream in which a child is on fire and says to his father, "Can't you see I'm burning?"

A painter she knew painted fire over all his finished paintings. There was something in it, she had to admit. Coffee came close and then she gave it up on account of a tricky bladder.

The husband read aloud about the man with the stiff leg, who didn't help bury the dog he'd accidentally killed. The man with the stiff leg cited his leg as a reason for not shoveling. The husband added ginger to the peanut sauce.

The wife had that thing and then she misplaced it. And found smudges on the windows. Aphids. On the hibiscus. Who wants an oversized plant with yellow blossoms when it introduces pests to an otherwise peaceful living space.

The wife walked up and down the hill behind the house, carrying one word at a time to the hilltop then dropping it over the ledge. She believed in breaking syllables out of their molds and mosaicking them all together again. It was the only way to get the thing back. That's what she said. Smash smash.

The people clanked cocktail glasses and called it fun. And sometimes a few of the dead showed up at the windows. In the dark. They scratched at the glass and both the husband and the wife saw them and waved. The dead seemed to know the texture of the thing.

The wife washed pots after dinner wearing gloves. The thing stirred in the air around her, generated in the way her digits moved in their rubber coverings. She had to admit she no longer knew how to eroticize a conversation. She liked to stand an egg in a nickel-sized hole in a cutting board and watch it. A little crooked. And set objects beside it. A candle holder. A ball point pen. A toy car. A blue shoe.

"What does anyone learn worth learning?" she called into the open refrigerator. She thought cold captured sound better. The husband didn't agree. He held his hands inside pot holders over his ears. "Let us not undervalue small signs," Freud said in his second lecture on psychoanalysis. A grain of cooked rice on a black stove top. Another aphid on a windowsill.

An old woman said to the wife, "You are late. Or you are early." And, "Trees leave space between their canopies intentionally."

"Sit over there," the wife told the old woman, "I don't like the smell of your urine. You are dehydrated. Obviously."

Will she, seeking out the seedpod of alive, refrain from touching what or whom she longs to touch? "What is desire," the husband said, "but the compulsion to transgress."

Portrait

On Monday, sitting in bed, having just finished the
last word, repelled, of the novel she was reading, she
knew she needed to locate herself more variously or she'd
end up frozen in a frame, her whole existence a single
image, head and torso surrounded by pillows and a
headboard. So Tuesday, when the sun hit the newly
exposed bank of excavated earth next door, she went to
the neighbor's backyard and stood beside a trailer, the
kind that hooks to the back of a truck, and took a
picture of herself. Wednesday she traveled to the bus
station and stood before the ticket booth for thirty
minutes without purchasing a ticket, telling the ticket
salesperson not to mind her, she was just expanding her
horizons. Thursday she drove to a local funeral home at
dawn and sat on the stoop, the doors locked shut behind
her for hours yet, and watched her breath in the cold
morning air. Friday she walked to the circle at the end of
her street and looked back at her house from there,
looked and looked and looked until the house moved far
far away in both space and time. She kept looking until

she could sense a landline attached to the wall by the refrigerator once again, and then she stood there longer, listening, as the phone rang and rang and rang in the empty kitchen.

WHO GOES THERE? NAY, ANSWER ME

I was resting my tibia, fibula, talus, ligaments and whatnot on a piece of stuffed furniture named for an ancient empire, my posture the slope of an egg laid the long way, and piecing together small black symbols with my eyes, as I often do, though for reasons I forgot years ago, when I heard wheels on gravel.

"For me? Have they come for me? Who are they?" I had a fleeting desire for them, whomever they might be, to exude erotic energy in my direction.

Instead, you guessed it, the well-dressed humans sharing doomsday literature. "Have you seen this one?" the man asked, pointing to a hand descending from clouds. I always offer them comestibles, though my cupboards are bare, since odds are on my side they'll refuse. I live for risks.

Something, my imitation of *Ardipithecus ramidus* perhaps, sent red blood cells swimming the streams in me and woke up all kinds of neurons until I found myself thinking of you. My, how you could sink into a sea of scribbles back in the day!

And remember how you had that Hamlet disease where you kept lying about seeing your dead father, especially when you wore dress shoes in the rain. But why did you favor such thin ties? And have you sought chiropractic for your syntax?

Stand, I say, wherever you are. Unfold yourself and send signals this way if I'm not a Gorgon you keep shackled in your heart shack.

IN SERVICE

Bill, who loves his name because it calls to mind
shore birds and restaurant tallies and envelopes with their
transparent windows stacked in mailboxes, because it
puts at ease numerous recovering alcoholics, reminding
them with its one simple syllable that a world of their
peers is always within reach at a nearby church basement
or high school cafeteria or hidden conference room at a
super-sized grocery store, because it was passed down to
him not from his somewhat lead-brained father, a man
who pooh-poohed all matters literary, deeming them
inconsequential for their lack of statistical relevance, but
from his grandfather on his mother's side, a man of such
eloquence and grace who once, on the day in fact of
Bill's birth, delivered a eulogy for Adrienne "Suzy"
Mante, niece of Marcel Proust, Bill's favorite writer and a
novelist of both literary renown and continuously
unfolding grammatical wizardry as well as singular
wisdom, or at least Bill thinks, since he has indeed been
reading and rereading, three pages at a time, Proust's
works daily for the last 1,435 days, a project he began in

a flash of inspiration during a visit to an empty chapel in Illiers-Combray on his 33rd birthday, the birthday on which the book had been given to him as a gift from that same namesake grandfather who'd died only ten days later so that now, as Bill reads his three daily pages, he often reflects on the fact that, had his grandfather died before his birthday, he, Bill's grandfather, may never have given Bill the gift of this book that has, in the last 1,435 days, so changed his life, word by word, and Bill might therefore never have begun the process of writing a novel of his own, a novel begun as it was with an image that came back to him only recently but which he'd first seen in that chapel on his 33rd birthday, the image being of a man with a hole through his center, the image which somehow led Bill to discover in himself a similar hole, the size of a cantaloupe and like one as well, in being not perfectly round, and through which, in Bill's daily life, so much has passed – air, water, the occasional men's black shoe, small birds, maple leaves, desires, griefs, old loves, photographs, the lines of poems scribbled on bits of paper and crunched up then tossed through, helped along by Bill's most beloved friend Stephen, who does whatever he can in service to Bill and by extension in service to Bill's novel, since he not only loves Bill with a devotion that stretches back to infancy but is also a reader of appetite and appreciation who senses that helping Bill to complete his novel will also result in a deeply satisfying read for himself, and so it is that on Tuesday, Stephen scrawls out a little poem by the French poet Jean Follain, a ten-line poem in which is depicted a map of Asia on which insects make their way from the Indus to the Amour River, and folds the paper into an airplane which he then flies, skillfully, steadily, through the cantaloupe-sized hole in his good friend Bill and beyond, and they both watch as the paper airplane poem continues its flight across the park where they have been walking and, lifted by a breeze, is carried to where it lands in an abandoned robin's nest at the heart of a now leafless red maple right beside another paper airplane of unknown origin which may or may not have anything written on it, but, being high up in the maple's branches, will probably never be examined, at least not by Bill or Stephen, neither of whom is a very good climber.

MORNING LETTER

I was just sitting at the kitchen table looking up the population of Lipetsk (447,000 in 1988, the year my beaten-up dictionary was published) when it occurred to me I ought to install a listening post if I hope to move forward with any of my more involved plots. Are you interested in fulfilling the position?

About ten minutes ago, my husband poured my nearly full cup of coffee down the drain. Snow makes leaving him today unlikely. Tomorrow there'll be rain and a host of other reasons to stay. Thus do we age amicably side by side in a couple of comfortably furnished rooms where we rely on Samuel Beckett to restore electricity to the parts of us that appear to slumber too continuously.

It's more than likely there are fewer than forty more visits that anyone of our age who lives a few hours from their mother's town is likely to have with their mother if they still have a mother. Or anyone else.

Pen in hand, I often feel myself a ne'er do well. How about you?

Do you like to wear clothing the color of unripe olives?

Do you proudly not call yourself an omophagist?

If you practiced oneiromancy, would you predict the future using my dream from last night in which my therapist performed in a crowded bar playing a small cello at 10:30 pm? Would you agree that what was most remarkable is that she sat on a swing that hung from very long ropes and wore a blue skirt? She never wears skirts. What would you say of the old artist friend who appeared, wanting to show me elaborate mechanized sculptures he'd constructed from ancient wallpaper and gears given to him by someone named Lem?

I really want to work but I want the work to matter. Or make me say ooh once in a while.

Did you know that polecats have offensive anal scent glands?

I miss you. And that cup of coffee.

There's one thing of which I feel fairly certain. Neither you nor I will ever witness the fleshy-snouted saiga in its natural habitat. Would it be worth our saying we'd like to?

MR. LEOPOLD

Mr. Leopold's planet is off kilter. Actually, it isn't a planet at all but a small plot of land with a bungalow built smack in the middle, like a cut glass bowl filled with peppermints or pistachios set smack in the center of a coffee table. The plot is a small piece, of course, of a larger planet, but what does Mr. Leopold orbit?

Mr. Leopold spends a high percentage of his waking hours in a basement; last calculation had it at 39%. Of what is that 39% comprised? Besides a cigarette at frequent though irregular intervals, there's insulation to inhale and dust and dehydrated something or other that collects on the concrete floor, looking like foam but more solid and gritty to the touch. Mr. Leopold orbits several large pieces of paper laid on the floor on which he lays down paint using scrub brush, sticks, cigarette butts, and his fingers. It's possible Mr. Leopold believes his true self or Jesus or Buddha or Dr. Faustus or Beethoven will one day appear in the splotches and swirls and smears of paint, anointing him or explaining to him the secret of perpetual motion. Why Mr. Leopold should need this information is uncertain.

In general, Mr. Leopold prefers to remain unaccompanied.

Sometimes Mr. Leopold imagines himself Marcel Proust and composes scenes in which a young man is berated by an older, distinguished gentleman with a small, red mouth and little black teeth who will later ruin himself for a Polish violinist. Mr. Leopold doesn't so much paint or write such scenes. Rather, he keeps the vision in his mind while he goes about preparing a stew or playing guitar, thus imbuing whatever he does with the sense of Proust's narrative and psychological pulses.

People in his town often smile when they encounter Mr. Leopold.

Often, he can be seen waving to people who don't appear to exist. He dresses smartly in trousers and a fur-lined coat and scrubs the paint from beneath his fingernails. Sometimes he misses a bit on his nose or earlobe. He forgets to look at himself.

These public encounters constitute only about 13% of Mr. Leopold's waking life, what with laundry and bathing and trips to the toilet and cemetery. Sometimes Mr. Leopold believes in music and the futility of love and inhales paint and is utterly content. Other times he plants tulips and weeps for what will never be.

In the very rear of Mr. Leopold's yard, a cluster of chrysanthemums has grown unruly, leggy, crazy every autumn with yellow.

GEORGINA LLOYD-ATKINSON

Having been born into a hyphenated surname, Georgina became, willy-nilly and without effort at first, though eventually with real determination, a consummate hyphenator. She found every opportunity to hyphenate absolutely ring-a-ding and razzle-dazzle, and she'd be sure to say so to whomever was listening. Indeed, over time she lived a life so well-ordered as to capitalize on any situation that made room for her linguistic peculiarity. When hungry for a sandwich, she'd never ask for a hero or sub or grinder but would always say, "Well, I could just kill for a poor-boy sandwich right about now." When she moved out of her parents' home and was furnishing her bedroom, she searched far and wide in consignment shops until she found just the right bow-front chest of drawers. Years later, when she was married and her husband occasionally mumbled, she reprimanded him for being so flannel-mouthed, and she never ironed her blouses or even linen dresses so as to provide herself with opportunities to explain away her wrinkles by saying she conserved energy through the rough-dry method of laundering. She set out on a regular schedule of night walks all the year round so as to be able one day to claim she'd spotted, or even heard, a saw-whet owl, she studied the local flora in order that she might make the acquaintance of a purple-fringed orchis, and despite her holier-than-thou attitude and keen sense of justice, she secretly delighted when corrupt politicians got away scot-free. She was, on occasion, accused of being strait-laced and rose-colored in her outlook, having intentionally cultivated such qualities so as to hear herself so described by others, thereby feeding her obsession on another level. During one Memorial Day parade she arranged to ride alongside a local automobile enthusiast in his 1938 bubble-top Coupe-de-Ville, and though she hardly knew the man, she pretended to be all palsy-walsy with him, even going so far as to tell him that whatever anyone else said of him, she could tell he was no perpetual buck-passer, no sirree!

IT's REALLY FUN HERE, EVEN IN A PANDEMIC

This is a new thing I do. I pile books into a really high tower beside me on the sofa, give them a little push, and let them topple and fall open. Then I tell the story of how my husband went to the grocery store for lettuce or to get the oil changed, inserting words from the pages of the open books into the telling. In such a way do our small rooms fill to bursting with erotic energy and women named Ingrid and Jane.

THE COAT

It's a Saturday in mid-January and very cold, 19 degrees with a wind chill of three degrees, and the husband has just gotten a new winter coat, which isn't really new. It's a new used winter coat, meaning it is new to the husband. And when he puts it on, he says to his wife that he feels sort of like a superhero. His feeling superhero-ish, his wife understands, is because even though the coat is thick and warm and puffy, it is also fairly lightweight, so when he and his wife go out for their walk, which they are doing now, he feels warm in his new coat, but he also feels a spring in his step because he is comparing how he feels in the new coat to how he felt in his old coat, which not only had a broken zipper but also was heavy and weighed him down when he walked. Now he feels he can walk farther and faster and maybe even save people from oncoming enemy bicyclists or renegade toy poodles or labradoodles on the path where he and his wife are walking.

He also feels a little like a dead man, he says, by which his wife can't tell whether he means he feels dead because the coat belonged to a man who is now dead, or if he feels like the man whose coat it was who is now dead, by which he might mean that he feels older, since the man whose coat it was was 94 when he died, and maybe he feels more educated since the man whose coat it was had a Ph.D. and earned numerous awards and honors for his scientific research whereas the husband has only an associate's degree.

The wife likes the way her husband looks in his superhero dead man's coat. It is gray and puffy and has a hood with fur around its edges, and even though the husband isn't wearing the hood, the way it bunches up, the fur makes a sort of collar, and his face looks sweet and young peeking out from that fur collar. And he is smiling and looks truly happy and energetic and brave like a superhero. As they walk along in the cold on the path, side by side, the wife begins to feel faint and wants to fall into the husband's arms but she doesn't. She keeps walking and she doesn't say anything, but she can feel herself falling in love with her new dead man superhero husband.

IOWA

Our family friend, who was my 2nd brother's godfather, had a thriving dental practice in Des Moines, Iowa. He also had a tough-talking ice-cube-chewing wife named Betty, two adopted children, one of whom, a son – a nihilist at the age of ten – would grow up to take over the dental practice, the other of whom, a daughter, would develop Huntington's disease and need full-time care by the time she turned twenty, and they all lived in a three-story, eighteen-room house with a heated swimming pool and an extensive gun collection. One summer our family of seven drove all the way to Iowa from Connecticut in a station wagon with no air conditioning to visit the dentist and his family. While in Iowa, we mainly stayed in the air-conditioned house and shot pool in the pool room, watched TV and played Candy Land with the then four-year-old daughter, and occasionally tiptoed, holding our breath, into the gun room, a largish room with glass cases devoted entirely to guns – shotguns, handguns, guns you had to cock, semi-automatic rifles – and ammunition. I think there were even a couple of grenades there but I might be making that up. When we did leave the house, we traveled to Lake Panorama, a man-made lake where we swam and water skied and which was hugely disappointing because it was extremely muddy and because the view did not live up to its name, a word I'd just learned that year from my fourth-grade literature textbook. A few afternoons we drove with the men to remote places where the dentist, his brother-in-law, and my brother, who was his godson, could shoot skeet while my sister and father and I sat in the air-conditioned car and drank sodas for hours. Since the dentist was our brother's godfather, he paid special attention to that brother. In fact, you might say the whole trip was intended to solidify their bond. While the wife chewed ice and smoked and we wondered what skeet were, our brother adopted a skill set foreign to the rest of us, who preferred reading stories and eating ice cream to learning the differences in types of ammo and the relative power of a 12 vs. 20-gauge shotgun. Since that time, much has happened, including (before both of their deaths) a falling out between our father and the dentist, and a trend of mass shootings in schools and other public spaces in our country. My siblings and I are all mostly a little haunted by that room at the heart of that house at the heart of this country, the nihilist son has carried on his father's dental practice with even more success than his father, and our fathers have both died. And that is why, though most members of our family adhere to a strict albeit unarticulated policy of refraining from any but the slightest reminiscence, and none of us is likely ever to posit a connection between our collective past and any of our present emotional or psychological well being, we all will, when traveling, select that route along which we can maintain the furthest possible distance from Iowa.

THE MAN WHO WAS AFRAID OF POETRY

A man was in his kitchen late one afternoon, slicing zucchini for a pasta dish he planned to make for dinner. He sliced the zucchini into thin wheels, enough wheels for an entire traffic jam of miniature automobiles. Does anyone say automobile anymore, as in, "Darn, my automobile has a dead battery." He stopped slicing when he noticed, tucked behind the bottles of olive oil and vinegar that lined his countertop, a poem, about ten or twelve lines long, probably 12-point font, on bright white paper. He froze. Fear made the hair on his forearms stand up. It shut the doors to both Broca's and Wernicke's rooms in his brain. Like many before him, at such moments he wished only to be rid of or even kill that which he feared. He considered grabbing for the broom and swatting at the poem. But the broom, used as it was for sweeping floors, was dirty and he didn't want any of that dirt to hit the counters or the wall against which the poem leaned, or to get anywhere near the zucchini. He felt his heart pound in his chest and his arms began to hurt from their sudden rigidity. He closed his eyes, knife in hand, and became more aware of the heft of the knife. Could he stab the poem? Again, there was the problem of the wall. Perhaps he could put on gloves and pinch the poem by a corner, lift it and pierce it with the blade tip. Or maybe he could avoid violence by calling in his friend Mary, who was very brave and never, as far as he knew, ran from any literary object. He felt certain she would help. She'd lift the poem, barehanded, eyes open, and probably read it aloud to him. She wouldn't laugh at him, wouldn't say, "What! You're afraid of that little thing??" Instead, she might say, "Look. Don't be afraid. It's quite friendly. See? It has plums in it and absolutely no teeth."

It Takes Years of Work

Alice Parker claimed one kind of damage and had five boyfriends. "One second," she said, not shouting, and Jean smeared the view of the storm with her life. Jean does what she can when she has the chance.

Alice Parker believed in recording everything.

"Why would anyone fear resting?" Jean asked, turning away from the voice-activated device.

"On the surface of things, style emerges without intent" was the kind of thing Alice Parker liked to play back.

I watched them every opportunity I got. Me and my dog, who is expert at roaming unleashed. We're writing a guidebook on the habits of select neighbors. We'll mail it by regular post.

We like blue metal boxes and the things Alice Parker considers compassionate. She is so far our best seller.

In Large Part

In the book I'm reading a young man tries to crack his teeth by swishing a mouthful of ice water and then throwing back slugs of hot coffee.

In the book I'm reading it's time to take a rest. And I am fifty years old. And bones float inside the bodies of dolphins.

In the book I am reading someone is not smoking. And a body makes a decision. And someone's job is to not get killed. And someone else sees a love of death in someone else's eyes.

In the book I'm reading someone else's job is to go to an elegant dinner. And someone named Mrs. Hotano takes forty dollars from the table in the hall. And a fountain yields dead earth worms. And she asks me with her hands to stay away.

In the book I'm reading the floors are badly cleaned. And in large part, we are meant to heal each other.

COMPLETE

Some people, though it isn't readily apparent to those around them, are actually two people. Sometimes this is the result of having, like Robert Frost, come to where two roads diverged in a yellow wood. Realizing that they cannot take both and remain one traveler, such people, through indecision or a sense of entitlement, decide that they will become two travelers in order to take both roads. So they become two people, each of whom marries a different person and lives in a house, often with children or a dog, and they go back and forth, changing hats and scarves and sometimes shoes in between so as to keep straight their identity in each house. They get work in sales or other occupations requiring frequent travel. In such cases, the already complicated situation tends to become more and more complicated the further down each road the two travelers travel. In other cases, often as the result of trauma, one person becomes two or more people in what the DSM 5 calls dissociative identity disorder. In such cases, two or more distinct identities are present, each with its own relatively enduring pattern of perceiving, relating to, and thinking about the environment and self. Such persons rarely derive great benefit from their condition, but their stories have made for interesting TV shows. Other times, it happens that in utero there are twins, one twin doesn't make it, and that twin gets absorbed into the surviving twin, without anyone noticing, in what is called vanishing twin syndrome. Some such twins carry a physical attribute, or even a whole other DNA, originally destined for their twin, but again, no one knows this. In Plato's *Symposium,* Aristophanes explains that in the beginning of time, people did not exist in single bodies as we do now but, rather, were pairs joined at the shoulder. There were three types of these pairs, and since they were always together – two males, a male and a female, or two females – they were never lonely. But then the humans did something to offend Zeus and he cut them apart as punishment. As Aristophanes explains it, because of this, all people wander through life looking for the person who will complete them since in the beginning we were two, not one. Sometimes, the people who are still two, the ones who absorbed their twin, do not know it, but because they are already two, they have trouble in love because they are not especially lonely and are therefore not looking to complete themselves. They want something else in love, though they're not sure what. All of this happens unconsciously and these people who are already two people don't even know it. Also, occasionally, they find themselves purchasing a red sweater or faux snakeskin boots that are totally not their style.

Scary Story

A woman answers her telephone. Who is it, she asks, suspecting it is her past, its thick shoulders all hunched, teeth in need of brushing, desires growing out all over its body like bent wire sculptures.

Cusp

I began the day with a problem. I was trying to come up with just the right shape to help me describe and therefore contemplate the complex nature of a particular relationship. Since that particular relationship was perplexing me, I decided to start by discovering the shapes of other, less perplexing relationships as I imagined their shapes would be more obvious. Approaching the problem in this way, I landed, naturally, on my relationship with my husband since it plays such a central role in my daily life and is, generally speaking, pleasing. Without much forethought I quite readily pictured my relationship with my husband as a giant tooth, a molar with its not flat tabletop and its big roots for legs. More particularly, I pictured it as a maxillary first molar, but much larger than an ordinary human maxillary molar. Because of how prominent a space this relationship occupies in my life, I reasoned that this molar needed to come from or fit into an enormous mouth, like King Kong's mouth. I pictured the enamel over the enormous crown of this enormous molar, the proportion of crown to what exists below the gum line, the roots anchoring themselves and the blood vessels and nerves inside the root canal. I pictured the pulp cavity and the surrounding dentin, the hard, dense bony tissue that forms the bulk of the tooth. The more I thought about us, the more clearly I could understand our cusps, our ridges and pits and furrows. I began to think it possible we had created, in coming together, a molar that featured something like a metaphorical cusp of Carabelli, in dental lingo a fifth cusp, which is actually a tubercle, made only of enamel, an eminence first described in 1842 by Georg Carabelli, court dentist to the Austrian emperor Franz.

My relationship with my husband, like the first maxillary molar, is detailed and has a lot under the surface. And it has not only ornament but functionality, like chewing. As in, we chew a lot. Together. We chew a lot of evenings together. For instance, sometimes we sit on our sofa by the fire and chew on the dark just outside our windows. Sometimes we go outside at night and chew on the sky itself. We chew moonlight and the dark between stars. Other times we go out early and chew sunrises on the marsh. We chew foxes and great blue herons and ice like torn fabric on the surface of the marsh grass. We're like grazers, basically. We chew the pages of books, we chew Proust in Balbec with his grandmother and the little gang of girls and their bicycles, one of whom leaps over the head of an octogenarian, and a year later we chew on the narrator's grief. We chew Thomas Mann and sometimes a little philosophy, and we chew poetry. The human mouth produces something like 25,000 quarts of saliva in a lifetime, enough to fill a couple of swimming pools and to continuously protect the teeth from bacteria that cause decay, and we need that kind of thing, my husband and I, we need protection from ennui and existential angst, and we do our best to get it. And still, we suffer some decay here and there. But mainly we take care of our molar, we brush and floss and walk and communicate and read spiritual books and meditate and occasionally seek counsel from experts in the care of such things.

But that other, problem relationship, after all my contemplation of the molar that is my relationship with my husband, I still couldn't decide on a shape for it. It is certainly multi-faceted, which again suggest molars, but one cannot compare all of one's relationships to teeth, and it isn't really a diamond either, diamonds being sort of cliche and too expensive at the same time. Was it like a thimble? Don't those usually have lots of little indentations, little dimples. Would hundreds of little dimples be a good metaphor for complexity and beauty and bumps in the road? The earliest known thimble dates back to the Han Dynasty in ancient China and was discovered during the Cultural Revolution in a lesser dignitary's tomb. If my relationship with this other person were a thimble, then perhaps the historical element was key. The changes we had gone through, improvements and brassinesss and variation in terms of relation to numerous fingers throughout time, numerous threads and mends and replacements, all of those aspects might speak to the as yet un-narrated story of our long and sometimes painful interaction. I got to thinking how thimbles could protect since that is their primary function, to protect the finger that stitches and mends and creates. But they could also be inverted to form a little cup from which one could presumably sip the rarest of pleasures in increments not entirely satisfying but having to suffice. But I never decided conclusively enough to be able to deepen my understanding or cement the slippery body of it all in place, and then I gave up for the time being since I had to get ready to go to the dentist.

Later, when I returned from the dentist, I got to thinking that maybe for my husband's and my next anniversary, I could hire a designer or furniture maker to construct a maxillary molar-shaped table for two out of some brightly colored durable resin, and I could put it on our deck where in summer we might sit under an umbrella and drink our coffee. Of course, when I presented the table to my husband, I would explain its significance, since otherwise he might not appreciate the table and might think it a strange anniversary gift. But then I got to thinking it might not make such a great table since the top of the tooth, if it were to be accurate, wouldn't be flat enough on which to set our coffee cups. So I thought, instead, I could get the designer to design a molar-shaped ottoman, and then it wouldn't matter if the top of the crown had cusps and pits, yes, we could sit on the sofa in the evening and read our books or watch a movie and rest our feet on our shared, molar-shaped ottoman. Gertrude Stein and Alice B. Toklas had Picasso design cushions for two chairs and then Alice stitched the designs in needlepoint and the chairs were set in their living room at a little distance from each other. Knowing this made me feel that our ottoman would therefore connect us to Alice and Gertrude and the Paris of the early 20th century. But then I felt a little disappointed that we couldn't have seat cushions designed by Picasso, so I reasoned that our ottoman would be equally valuable to us since our molar represents our relationship. Still, if Picasso were alive and were willing to design anything for us, I'm sure I would opt for that, but then I would need someone to stitch the pattern in needlepoint, and then it hit me like a big ouch-to-the-fingertip inspiration that, yes!, then I could stitch the design in needlepoint using my thimble. In such a way, somehow, there came into focus a relationship between the two relationships I had been considering, and while I couldn't quite articulate that significance, I felt it to be important. I felt momentarily the connectedness of all relationships and a sense that each somehow supported the other. At this point, I looked up from my thinking and saw a woodpecker on an oak tree outside my window, its head bobbing, as woodpeckers' heads often do, and it seemed to me at that moment much like a sewing machine, the woodpecker, more so than like a person using a thimble and stitching by hand.

A Sad Tale

The husband who never stopped talking often narrated his own actions. "I'm going to throw the clothes in the dryer," he'd say and shuffle down the hallway to the door that led to the basement, and whoever happened to be present could hear his footsteps on the basement stairs, and seconds later the dryer door opening, the washer opening, clothes plopping bunch by bunch into the dryer, the dryer door closing and the dryer starting. Then his steps again, across the basement and back up the stairs, the door opening, the husband coming back down the hall to the kitchen where he might announce, "That's done. I think I'll change the music. I appreciate this Shostakovich, but it's very heavy," and then opening a kitchen cupboard, he'd say, "Want a snack? How bout an almond?" to his daughter, perhaps, who might be sitting on the sofa, reading, annotating a story by Joyce Carol Oates, a story in which the father never speaks at all, and the daughter reading the story might try her best to block out, "What're you reading? Is it any good? Where's your mother? I'm gonna go water the bonsai tree. I'm gonna find socks. Dmitri Karamazov's been accused of the murder, but I'm confused about these three thousand rubles. Want some ice cream?" If words worked like a large pencil eraser, his wife and child might only be rubber crumbs by now. "I'm gonna get my pajamas on, get ready for bed," he'd say to the rubbings on the kitchen table or on the living room floor. His daughter, the rubbings of her that remained, might lie on an open book on the sofa, and the husband who never stopped talking might walk by the book and say, "I think I'll make some tea. Green tea. With lemon. It's really tasty. You should try some."

A Happier Tale

Sometimes it would happen, perhaps on a Tuesday of no particular import, especially if she'd been suffering a bout of the literal, that Elizabeth would wake from an architecture dream only to feel, in a manner akin to how she felt when a dental assistant draped a leaded cape over her in order to x-ray her bicuspids, pressed with disappointment. Not that the dream itself would have disappointed. On the contrary, the dream would have followed a familiar and extraordinary pattern of discovery, Elizabeth wandering down the hallway of her own conventional home to find a door which she would open to a room she'd never before seen, often an ancient earthy kitchen with fire-fed ovens or a spacious but warm room, two walls composed almost completely of windows, overlooking woods and a stream or a small waterfall, well-crafted built-in bookshelves on either side of a stone hearth in which a fire gently blazed. What disappointed Elizabeth was waking to the shoddy cabinets of her own kitchen, the ceiling which seemed designed to box thought. Not that the walls hadn't original artwork, not that odors of cumin and garlic, of jasmine rice or of morning coffee didn't infuse the air with nourishment for more than the body, but the lack of a single black porcelain doorknob or molded cornice could get Elizabeth very down. But one Tuesday, very much like the others, Elizabeth awakened from yet another architecture dream. Who could say the difference? Was it the book she'd been reading before she fell asleep? Was it having eaten a crisp Macintosh and overhearing a spiritual teacher? Was it the cool autumn air or the word *clarity* which had popped intermittently into her consciousness for days on end? The dream had differed slightly. The house hadn't been her own, the rooms had been plentiful, one more pleasing than the next, and it had been a public space, intended for whoever wished to read on one of its rich red chairs or gather with friends at one of its heavy wooden tables for a dinner prepared by many mysterious hands. Elizabeth opened her eyes. She opened the eyes in all the rooms of her psyche, all the rooms of her spleen and her heart and her skin, and she smiled, breathed, gave thanks for the architect.

A Good Length for a Story

In the year 1847 Tolstoy kept in his diary a list of *Rules for Developing the Will.* One of the challenges Tolstoy faced in adhering to his own rules, particularly his rule of eating in moderation, and nothing sweet, was his love of raisins. Apparently, Tolstoy couldn't stop eating raisins. Mr. Leopold has read about Tolstoy's rules, which also include walking an hour every day and getting up at 5, both of which Mr. Leopold adheres to himself, but without referring to either as a *Rule*.

But Mr. Leopold can see nothing wrong with eating sweets, especially raisins. He is of the opinion that certain moments in life seem more plump, more sweet, more concentrated with meaning and feeling and memory and imagination than other moments, and he thinks of these moments as raisins (or perhaps dried blueberries, of which he is also particularly fond). He associates the experiencing of such moments with the eating of raisins and therefore believes it good to eat raisins.

Mr. Leopold appreciates raisins, and when he

compares them to grapes, he feels that while grapes are sweet and cool and light, like joyful, light moments, often experienced in the company of groups of others, raisins are compressed moments, usually experienced in solitude and when one is present, open, and operating at optimal experiential capacity, or perhaps in the company of one other person when and only when that person is also particularly present.

In fact, Mr. Leopold has been noticing recently varying degrees of presence. When he feels himself to be particularly present, Mr. Leopold wishes to eat the little fruits of those moments with wild abandon. Conversely, he has noticed that sometimes he can be present one moment, though perhaps not deeply present, and then, as if there's been a sudden change in barometric pressure, he can vanish, and he can tell that the words he is thinking or speaking are words he has thought or said many times before. He sees them running on a ticker tape across the bottom of a screen in his brain, a screen tuned into the station he most often tunes into. He senses that his eyes get a flat look, but fiery at the same time.

It sometimes happens that Mr. Leopold is with a companion and he longs to remain present with his companion, wherever the conversation goes. He sees the two of them, ice skating side by side, gliding along perfectly parallel even though the parallel is serpentine, the ice lit up by the moon, their scarves trailing behind them, the two of them rarely lifting their feet, propelling themselves instead by a swaying motion of hips and legs.

But then it can happen here too, and suddenly either Mr. Leopold or his companion has disappeared. Sometimes Mr. Leopold has the sensation of watching himself, mid-conversation, seem to hop on a motorcycle and zoom down the road of whatever feeling or memory is evoked in him by his own speech. If the feeling is anger, then the angrier the story makes him, the faster the motorcycle zooms away.

Mr. Leopold never quite knows what to do when it is his companion instead of himself who hops on their motorcycle mid-conversation. He doesn't generally try to call his companion back because most motorcycles, even metaphorical ones, are loud, especially when they accelerate. Plus, he knows from experience that the person riding generally wears a helmet, which further convinces Mr. Leopold that his calls won't be heard.

The other day, in the midst of such a moment, when Mr. Leopold was trying to figure out how to handle this sudden departure, it occurred to him that he might give himself a gift intended to assist him in such situations. At first he thought maybe a motorcycle, for obvious reasons, but that seemed a bit extravagant. Mr. Leopold hasn't a lot of money, and anyway, what he was after was something that would help him in brief moments such as the one he was experiencing. So then he thought, how about a book. Books are always good presents.

Yes, Mr. Leopold thought, he would get a small book he could carry on his person, designed for times of a companion's sudden departure, a book with very little stories in it. The book would be small enough to fit inside a shirt pocket, and slender, only about 30 or 35 pages max, and he could read one of the little stories in there, one teeny sweet bite at a time, chewing and swallowing slowly, until his companion turned their motorcycle around, zoomed back, slowed down, stopped and dismounted, parked the bike and removed their helmet. Whatever amount of time that took is how long each little story would be. Yes, Mr. Leopold thought, that would be a good length for a story.

Perfect Marcia

A wife walks into a kitchen where she finds her
husband hunched over the sink, hands pot-holdered,
straining boiling water from a pot. He is about to mash
potatoes for a shepherd's pie for their dinner that
evening. Careful to keep out of his way because she
knows he gets grumpy if anyone enters the kitchen when
he's cooking, the wife tries to make herself invisible via
silence and keeping to the periphery as she fills the
teakettle, grabs a blue ceramic mug from one cupboard
and a teabag, ginger, from another. She says not a word
while her husband begins his mashing. Still, watching
him, she anticipates his need for milk, and as the
thought of his needing milk comes to her, it is
accompanied by a memory concerning the potato
mashing practices of the stepmother of an old friend.
The stepmother, whom the wife met only once, at the
friend's wedding some 27 years ago, but about whom the
wife heard many stories, didn't use butter or milk in her
mashed potatoes, substituting fat free chicken broth for
both so as to lessen the calorie and fat content, a fact

which the friend, who died many years ago due to complications from alcoholism, found both annoying and ridiculous, referring to her stepmother in the telling of this and many other stories as "perfect Marcia." Saying nothing of her memory, the wife hands the husband the milk container, pours her hot water, and leaves the room, relocating to the sofa in the living room with book and steeping tea. Some moments pass. Then, the wife hears the husband begin to sing a song, one he's just made up, or is making up as he goes, a song that features the name of the friend of whom the wife had just been thinking. The husband knows nothing of the way Marcia makes mashed potatoes.

THE SHAPE

In the days after the visiting aged mother leaves, the daughter looks at the spaces the mother has left behind. There's a space in the shape of the mother on the sofa, beside the end table and the reading lamp. The daughter can't sit there because the space in the shape of the mother won't undo itself. A space in the shape of a book is suspended before the shape of the mother and the shape of the mother turns its pages, one after another, all day and night. There's a space in the shape of the martini glass from which the mother drinks her daily 5 o'clock cocktail. A martini glass takes up a lot of space on a shelf in a cabinet. It's an inconvenient shape for storage. And though a space that lacks the concreteness of being is far less awkward than an actual glass, it asserts itself still with a certain prominence, a bossiness, haughtiness, a flashy elan. It pontificates from its silence, especially if it has a complicated history attached. The space in the shape of the martini glass left behind in the mother's absence multiplies itself. It hangs from the ceiling repeatedly like a string of party lights. It lines itself up on the coffee table and weaves like a row of drunk paper dolls. It dances across the kitchen floor at 4:45 with the cat who wants his dinner. All the while the space in the shape of the mother in the den makes itself small where it sleeps on the sofa, sheets neatly tucked about its shrinking self.

Love Story

The first thing you'll notice is that he always backs in. It appears he's readying for a getaway. But from what? Also, he's good at giving things up. Smoking. Drinking. Peanut butter sandwiches. TV and tortellini. And he's steadily improving his evening crossword performance. Which I would argue follows from his having taken up gentle yoga.

You may also notice he knows no one named Ingrid. And that he plays the guitar left-handed when he plays it at all and will sometimes bore company with talk of sled dogs in Alaska, a subject he knows nothing about.

Once, he said to me, "This is not the Iditarod," by which he meant "Slow down."

Jean looked genuinely pleased. She loves it when anyone criticizes my pace.

"Is it true you find God boring?" he asked the postman.

He had poisoned the ants in the mailbox and immediately regretted it, but no one had wanted to retrieve the mail.

You'll notice he's not a good detective. Ask the neighbors who recently purchased a new used Chevy Impala.

On Valentine's Day he drives, I sit in the passenger seat. We roll along until we see cows on a hillside. He wears something French – *une chemise, les chaussettes, un caleçon*. I say, "All of us should visit a fishing lodge once in our life," and he agrees with me. He says, "It's essential to have gone angling for walleye in Ontario. Or muskie in the breathtaking Muskoka region."

We count the cows. The number will be useful later. We are patient for when it will be so.

THE JOYS OF READING

Though I read often and enjoy reading more than almost anything in life, I'm not very good at reading for information. In fact, I almost never do read for information, and when I do, the information is refused entry into the part of my brain where memory is created or stored. It's as if there's a guard house and a gate somewhere on the periphery of my brain, just on the other side of my eyes, and when a bit of information drives up in its car (it doesn't matter if the car is a beat up Datsun from 1972 or a brand new Lexus, or anything in between, like a 2011 Camry, a very popular car if ever there were one, or a Prius with a few life-affirming bumper stickers on its back bumper), the guard steps out of his guard house, looking officious, and asks for identification and other information. The guard is asking information of the information! Who is the information going to visit? Can the information prove it? How long does the information plan to stay? And because inevitably the gate is never opened and the information is not allowed to drive through, I am forced to take notes on whatever it is I am wanting to remember, a date for instance, or a statistic on women's earnings compared to men's in 2018 vs. 1998.

While I might expect not to be able to remember what year Martin Luther pinned his 95 Theses to the church door, or the distance from the earth to the moon, my condition, if that's what one would call it, persists even when the information in question delights me, such as what year Gertrude Stein moved to 27 Rue de Fleurus in Paris and when she stopped wearing those awful puffy Gibson Girl blouses and skirts that really didn't suit her and began wearing loose fitting, priestly looking robes. And what year Marcel Proust hired two boxes at the theater and threw a party for his friends, celebrating his retreat from social life to begin writing *In Search of Lost Time* in a fur coat in his bed under seven woolen blankets.

Recently, I got into trouble over my poor reading habits. My father-in-law, before he died at the age of 92, wrote a novel. He wrote the novel somewhere around the age of 89 and published it I think, though I can't recall for certain, when he was 90. I read the novel with great interest, in part because I was so impressed that one could write a novel at such an advanced age, since so many people talk about wanting to write a novel but never do, and also because I liked my father-in-law and wanted to experience his thinking in the way that a novel allows one to do, granting us access to parts of one's inner life that everyday conversation never does.

Whenever anyone went to visit my father-in-law,

who lived with his eldest son, my brother-in-law, this brother-in-law would quiz the visitor on information from the novel. He was of the belief that if you couldn't recall the information in the quiz, it was proof that you had lied and said you'd read the novel when in fact you hadn't. As is to be expected, now that you know of my reading disability, I could not recall the particular information since my focus in reading my father-in-law's novel had been on the story, on the way he'd adapted his personal life, including details of his children's lives, into his story. In particular, as I read, I became very interested in a love affair the protagonist, a definite stand-in for my father-in-law, has with a woman he meets in Florida while attending a baseball camp for senior citizens. I was enthralled with the love affair because in all the years I have known my father-in-law, he has never seemed to have any romantic relationships. My husband's mother, my father-in-law's only ever wife, died before I met my husband, some thirty years ago, and I wondered as I read if this fictional relationship, the one described in the novel, had indeed existed in life and if he had kept it from his family because he and all of his children had so beatified his wife/their mother and the institution of marriage itself that, even though she'd been dead thirty-plus years, he wasn't comfortable revealing to his children his affection for another woman. And so the novel became more interesting to me since he was indeed sharing the novel with them before he died, which meant that perhaps writing the novel was his way of letting them know he had indeed loved again. Who knows, maybe he wanted them to know that it was okay, were any of them to find themselves in a similar situation, being widowed long before one's own death, to love again. But because I focused on this emotional aspect of the novel and didn't know the detail my brother-in-law quizzed me on, he assumed I had lied about reading the novel. He even told me how he had found out that many people who said they'd read the novel really hadn't, and he said he knew this because they couldn't answer his question about a pooka.

Still, even though I failed my brother-in-law's quiz and am not about to try to convince him that I did indeed read my father-in-law's novel with interest, and even though I have difficulty reading for information, I love to read and think I actually excel at reading in some ways, including my ability to sink deeply into the world of whatever it is I am reading, to absorb the rhythm of the sentences and turns of mind of the writer or narrator, to engage with a range of emotional nuances to which the book grants me access.

There is one book I bought for myself several years ago while I was out Christmas shopping that I love very much and always keep close by. I don't mean I carry it with me, but it is often on my bedside table, or if not there, it's on my desk or the passenger seat of my car. Or sometimes, when I'm giving it a rest, I put it on a special spot on my bookshelf so that I can always find it with ease. The book is a short, squat collection of queer little stories with a strangely colored orangey pink cover with cream-colored lettering and the color scheme reversed on the spine written by a woman whose writing I only discovered when I picked up this book on a sale table in a bookstore that year when I was Christmas shopping because I was drawn to its shape and unusual color. And when I opened it there in the bookstore and read a few sentences, I fell immediately in love. I just had to have that book.

In this book there's a story about a woman who is a professor who fantasizes that she would like to marry a cowboy. She is, I think, a professor of literature who thinks a lot and one of the things she thinks is that she'd like to marry a cowboy because he'd be laconic and do cowboy things and not think too much because he'd know clearly what it was he needed to do in terms of saddling up his horse and roping the cows, and she thought, I think, that he'd have a lot of sky in his head, and open plains and clouds, big gray fast-moving clouds, and he wouldn't spend time questioning whether or not to wear his cowboy hat. I think I remember that his hat was one of the things she thought she might love about her cowboy husband, and his boots, and spurs if he had spurs, and who knows, maybe she'd discover her own hat. Not that she'd wear a cowboy hat per se but maybe she meant that she'd discover a clear sense of identity, as clear as a cowboy's, that she'd find something that suited her the way the cowboy's hat suits the cowboy. Heck, I don't really remember, but she liked to think of her cowboy even though she eventually married someone else who never even rode a horse.

About three years after I read the story about the

woman who fantasizes about marrying a cowboy, I read a story about a woman who is married to a man whose ex-wife is a professor who fantasizes about marrying a cowboy, and the woman in this story, which is a novel, wonders if, because the ex-wife has been offered a job, a professorship, in Texas or someplace like that, where there are numerous ranches and therefore cowboys, perhaps the ex-wife will really marry a cowboy after all. I came to read this novel, also by a woman writer, because I had read a different, later novel by her, a novel I loved which had an interesting structure borrowed from Kierkegaard's *Either/Or* which has a fictional introduction in which the fictional narrator tells the reader of his discovering papers in an escritoire he purchased from an antique shop whose windows he passed by each day. In the woman's novel, the fictional narrator of the introduction has discovered a series of journals written by a woman artist who came up with an elaborate system of journal writing, arranged according to topics with one journal for every letter of the alphabet so that the O journal for instance would include thoughts on the occult and orgasm and quotes by Flannery O'Connor, etc. Anyway, because I loved this book, and because, on completing reading it, I experienced what felt like lights turning on in various organs in my body, I decided I needed to read more of her work. So, I went to the library to find other novels by this same author, which is how I found the book in which the woman narrator is married to a man, and the man is friends with another man who is an artist, and each man has a son, the artist with the artist's wife, and the other man, the narrator's husband, with his ex-wife, the one who the new wife narrator remembers fantasized about marrying a cowboy.

Well, you can imagine how interested I became. I wondered how many readers had, like me, read both of these stories, and if so, how many had wondered if the writer of the second story, the novel, was indeed using details from real life about the writer of the first story to write her own story about a woman whose husband's ex-wife fantasizes about marrying a cowboy. Well, I did a little research, and it turns out the writer of the second story, the novel, is married to the man that the first writer used to be married to and it's possible that the second writer based her story, or that one detail in her story, which after all isn't that significant in the whole scheme of the novel, on the first writer's story, not her actual life. Or perhaps the first writer, though she writes fiction, uses her life in her fiction, and the second writer knows that. And then of course the second writer was using her own life in her fiction, since the narrator of the novel is the woman whose husband's ex-wife fantasizes marrying a cowboy, and it was all delightful for me to see, in a way, because I am interested in how much of one's life it is okay to use in one's fiction and not only that, how widespread the practice is. And not only one's own life but the lives of those who are close to one and those who were formerly close to them. And I also wonder how many people have shared this particular reading experience with me. Presumably, the husband of the second writer read her novel and recognized the reference to his first wife's story, if he read his first wife's story. It is also possible that he doesn't read his first wife's writing but that his second wife does, on the sly. Or that she reads it and tells him she reads it but that he says he just isn't interested. But I haven't looked into the dates and it might be that he was married to his first wife when she wrote the story about the cowboy, which makes it more likely he would have read the story. Unless of course he never reads anything that anyone he is married to writes, on some kind of principle. Did the first wife, the writer of the cowboy story, read the second wife's novel? Did she immediately recognize the reference to herself? Did she find it aggravating or flattering or humorous or some combination of all the above? Did the friends of the first wife who'd read her story years ago also read the second wife's novel, and did they see the connection or overlook those particular details, and if they noticed them, did they find the reference amusing or not amusing and does the story become more amusing rather than annoying the further removed the reader is from the first story, the story of the professor woman who thinks she'd like to marry a cowboy? I'm not sure I will ever know the answer to any of my questions concerning the readers of the inner circle, but what of other, more removed readers?

Thus far, I have not met a single person who has told me she has had this experience. I have not given up though. I did for instance, recommend the book of stories to a woman I happen to know already read the novel of the second wife. And it is possible that one day someone will happen to see the book I keep close at hand, the little squat book of stories, and he or she will leap into the story of how he or she read a story in that book about a woman who wanted to marry a cowboy and then, years later, read a novel by another woman and so on. We will strike up a friendship then, most likely, based on our shared delight in this reading experience. Or not. It is really impossible to foresee such things. In the end I find it pleasing that my appreciation of the work of these two women writers, both of whom have married the same man at some point in their lives, is what brought me to my discovery. It especially delights me because their writing styles differ so. In the first place, the difference is structural. One writes very short stories whereas the other writes full-length novels with very elaborate plot structures and narrative inventions. This difference in types of books has been explored in great length by Roland Barthes in a lecture series he gave called *The Preparation of the Novel*, though Barthes doesn't refer to a single work by a woman writer in his lectures but instead compares the differences between Pascal's little *Pensées* to Proust's seven-volume single *Work*.

The Reasons

A woman has a husband though the verb *has* troubles her. She's *had* him, as in been married to him, for a rather long time. It isn't like having a cat. Or like having zucchini soup for dinner. He's good looking but he can't do fractions. He's an excellent cook and he eats triple-decker sandwiches after dinner. She wonders how she ended up with this particular husband, there being, she imagines, many humans she might have married or lived with without marrying, or had children with, other than this one. It's a reasonable question, she thinks, how she ended up with this husband. She isn't romantic, doesn't believe they were somehow meant for each other, as in stars aligning and whatnot. The man who is the husband prefers to do as much as he can in the dark before dawn. He has a new hip, which he loves. He leaves windows open in winter because he opens them in the dark and then forgets he opened them and can't see that they are open. He reminds her that Proust's narrator kept Albertine prisoner, and maybe, his saying suggests, they should therefore rename their cat Albertine, even though their cat is male, since the husband thinks they are keeping the cat prisoner. Some of their friends think they are perfectly suited to each other. Others hit their foreheads with the heel of their hand at the idea of it. Some grimace. Others laugh. Some alternately grimace and laugh and then say, of course, of course. The woman wonders if her choosing this husband had anything to do with her father, whether it had to do with similarities between this man and her father. Their height is about equal. Her father liked mashed potatoes and so does this man. Her father was terrified of snakes, even cartoon snakes. Her husband falls closer to indifferent with regard to snakes but is often on the lookout for a kingfisher. The man she married believes their neighbor, an elderly woman who lives directly across from them, mistook a woman in a winter coat walking on their street for a coyote running across her yard. What happened is, the neighbor called to tell them to make sure their cat was inside. The cat is an indoor cat, though it has escaped on a few occasions, its escapes apparently having been witnessed by the neighbor. The neighbor had just seen a coyote run across her yard, she said, heading towards their place. In response to the neighbor's call, the woman went looking for the cat and found him asleep on a kitchen chair. The husband, who didn't bother looking for the cat, said he wasn't worried. He said he saw a woman on the street in a coat with a fur collar and that was probably what the neighbor saw. She probably saw that and thought it was a coyote, he said.

ORANGE

When she told me I reminded her of a *pika*, I knew she was lying. I'm not small for starters, I've not got rounded ears, and I've only one pair of incisors. Still, her saying so helped us to feel sexy with one another, which, it turns out, was what we were after, even if we'd had no idea about that when we first walked into that abandoned *mikvah*.

Language is like that sometimes. And I could see she had words packed in tight all over her hands and neck – small, 5-point font or smaller, perfectly formed Times New Roman letters inked there by some miraculously small printing device. I had to make my tongue into the finest pointiest point to lick the words located exactly in the center of that little indentation at the base of her throat, the hollow where her clavicle bones met. Orange, her skin read, right there in the center, a reddish yellow, round, edible citrus fruit. Glossing past the Old French and Latin origins, I tasted the word's Persian history, its Sanskrit *naranga* probably akin to the Tamil *naru* for fragrant, which it was, that word, there. Yes, I said, let me try that again.

BIRTHDAY

Over dinner he dabs at his mouth with his red
napkin, pauses, taps his fork to his temple, asks me why I
can't just act like I'm a law enforcement official and he a
criminal who I want to devour with passion despite his
criminality. That's a lot of layers of imagining for me. I
ask if we can't just talk about Thomas Mann some more.
It's not a lot of imagining for someone like me, he says.
How official an official do I need to be, I ask. Local
police? FBI? Special serial crimes investigator? Detective?
Sergeant? Private Investigator? What kind of education is
involved? I'm failing him, I can tell. Go have a cigarette
and recover, I say. And clear our plates. And snuff three
candles. And look for the cuffs.

Arizona

When Mr. Leopold visits his friend in Tucson, he keeps a list in his pocket of activities he wishes to perform. The first is to stroll hand in hand with his friend, mid-morning, the length of a lengthy alameda, a walk, shaded as by cottonwood trees, which are a type of poplar, or alamo. He wishes to do so while reciting, if he can recall it in its entirety, the sentence from *Ulysses* when Molly says she must clean the keys of the piano with milk. He wishes to recite this sentence since, well into it, Molly refers to fig trees in the Alameda Gardens, though her reference is to Gibraltar whereas Mr. Leopold is in Arizona.

Animal Behavior

Every morning the husband gets up early. After he goes down into the kitchen and makes coffee, the husband climbs back up the stairs and brings to his wife in bed a cup of coffee and a worry.

"I'm worried that the cat is eating too much."

"Is this my throat or my neck? I'm worried that I might have throat cancer."

"My shoulder hurts; I'm afraid I might have lung cancer."

"I'm worried that the transmission is going."

"I'm congested; I'm worried about my prostate."

"Can you smell the stove? I'm worried we're all gonna die."

"It's Christmas Eve. I'm concerned that the cat doesn't use his time well. He just stares at his bowl."

"I read online that stove pellets should be stored outside. I'm worried that they're giving off carbon monoxide."

"The car pulls a little to the right. Have you noticed that? I'm just worried that my neck, or my throat, is somehow related to this feeling of being RUN DOWN."

"I'm worried about the cat. He just sits there at the bottom of the stairs. I think he's unhappy. Imagine that, being an animal in a house."

Revival

She said the marriage was a dead thing. She said she'd poked it with a stick. It had felt, she said, much like a dead chipmunk she'd pushed off the side of the road with a different stick once, the dead heft of it traveling to her through the shortness of the stick.

She said she'd tried to revive it once with an orange. The marriage. One sweet slice at a time. Her fingers had gotten sticky and she'd licked them when no one was looking and wiped them on her corduroys.

She said she agreed with Freud that what is remembered in dreams is not what is most important but what is indifferent and insignificant. She said did I like roasted Brussels sprouts. She had some left over from yesterday's dinner.

She said what she'd most likely remember of the marriage was in which drawer they'd kept the pot holders. She'd torn her blouse the afternoon after she'd given her father's eulogy and when she asked the husband if he thought it could be mended he hadn't answered.

She said he roamed when he brushed his teeth and only stopped when he arrived at a window, which he'd open in all weathers. He seemed to need more air at such times. She had no plans for action.

She'd achieved ataraxy, she said, after years of teaching herself to stitch in the evenings.

She said the husband was lively and friendly and it was only the marriage itself that had become a rolled up carpet in the corner of a dusty back bedroom. A deflated football. A broken casserole. She said the tea in their teacups had grown cold.

She said the word *luncheon*, which had been popular in Nancy Drew's day, seemed to have gone by the wayside. Once, on an elevator in Osaka, she'd seen a Japanese man masturbate though she'd not wanted to. They had never eaten lamb, not once, she and the husband. After dinner she enjoyed turning off music.

She said she remembered standing by the shore listening to a creepy old man tell her things, but she couldn't remember what he'd said, only that she'd grown frightened and hopped on her bike and rode away fast.

She'd never liked the frightened giddiness one got from being dropped from a great height by an uncle. She'd not liked not being listened to. She'd not liked liver without having tasted it. She'd then tasted liver and disliked it even more.

She'd sufficiently appreciated too few paintings, she felt, to give an impromptu lecture on them.

An artist she knew had begun to paint fire. She stood by as he painted flames over all his finished paintings. She read a novel in which the young protagonist, having returned to England from Germany and teaching in a school in the north of London, can't understand how anyone can enjoy eating cheese.

She'd most often lived in second floor apartments. She'd once been late on her rent. Neighbors, she said, could make interesting subjects for the study of rhetorical strategies.

The husband had never recovered from their next door neighbor's building a metal garage. It wasn't the structure itself that bothered him, since it was red and barn-like, but the fact that the neighbor, who had needed their permission in order to gain approval from the zoning commission, had come to speak to them wearing his veteran's cap. Such blatant manipulation, the husband had proclaimed on many occasions. He woke screaming in the night saying yes to the neighbor. Happily, she said, he had broken his glasses and since she'd quit her job they hadn't money enough to replace them so he could no longer see the garage so clearly.

And then he'd read in Beckett about a man with a stiff leg who counted his farts in the course of a day, using math to come to a greater self-awareness, and who also had lost his sense of smell and could not therefore be reminded, years later, by the scent of lavender, of a woman who had whispered to him in the dark in her lavender garden.

On reading this, the husband's lost happiness had returned to him. As had his love. Which is the power of a few words sometimes, she said, especially when infused with the powerlessness and ignorance of the human condition.

YOU ARE ESPECIALLY ALIVE

Albedo, from the Latin *albus,* for white, refers to the reflecting power of a planet, satellite, or asteroid. However, as Mr. Leopold observes, some people also have measurable albedos. You, for instance, have an albedo nearly equivalent to snow.

Influences and Edibles

Where he stood on the other side of the screen door, having arrived to drive me away in a Chevy Vega, he wore well-worn clogs. That was new to me. Jeans so faded they were almost white, a shirt loose enough to send flames flickering from my ears.

There were a few moments then when my idiocy hid inside me like an Idaho potato with too many eyes.

We slapped our feet soles on puddled pavement later that night. And exchanged rhubarb recipes.

In the coming months we'd open cans of tuna, add red onion and mayo, then crunch crackers and lick each other's calculations.

He was holding us in place with controlled syntax. He was planting little patches of petunias in paragraphs pounded out on dead Uncle Joe's blue Smith-Corona. There were bike rides we were going to take. There was a movie we kept reinterpreting. There was an artichoke we were learning how to eat and it required we write sestinas.

There was Easter and the discomfort of lost faith and

ham.

One day when we were swimming in the swimming pool, a sibling flew off the roof and caused a splash that sent us into panko-encrusted existential questioning. And exoskeletal awareness. And we hadn't a dog. Nor had we a cat. And then he moved away to learn the law in a place with mountains. And his feet fanned out from years of slapping. Back home, I sat in pajamas, smudged prosody piled in my lap. And I didn't knit.

Menacing medical anomalies appeared in the years when we turned away from elongated winter shadows. And I began, for a brief time, to wear skirts. And we ate apricot jelly from our fingers and left bite marks on the blue binding of an old translation of Proust.

We had an idea we'd not count turkeys silhouetted in treetops on moonlit nights. We had a notion it'd be necessary at some point for a machine to breathe for one of us. We had a vague sense of what we'd do and not do in all kinds of empty corridors. To what music. And he occasionally licked his lips awkwardly as if looking for a word or becoming a wolf, and once I tried to sing for him while out walking on sand flats in Long Island Sound. And then his body grew lumps.

There were a few minutes one time that lasted several years and he began to look thin in the mirror.

And one day we ate vegetable soup and he photographed himself receding.

A NEW WAY OF WAVING

She is light-hearted and lets frozen peas thaw in her pants pocket. She looks all over the house and cannot find the reason dust makes her happy. She could chew on piecrust and repeat the word *cassette* and be asleep by dinnertime.

There is a sound originating in her shoulder. She tunes in. She closes her eyes and a fly hits a windowpane. She opens her eyes and the sound is no longer a sound but a hound is at the door, its eyes as big as egg yolks.

A man of Russian descent who used to write letters in fountain pen calls to her from miles and miles away through fog and snow and thirty years because he misses the owls in the way she speaks. She calls back, flapping as she does so, the flesh on her arms bumping against her bones.

HEART

Mr. Leopold collects blue things in a dusty cupboard in his mind. A bottle, a blue jay feather, a bit of thread, a cloth-bound dictionary. A dead fly, a ceramic coffee mug half full, a Bic pen cap. Along the gravel path that has been his life so far, he's also collected his experiences with words in books – lampshade, bedtime, church spire, Francois, asparagus. Also, the being in one's being in one's middle middle being, anima and animus and the unconscious and repressed and *utsuroi*. His collections, which include rooms, and books read in those rooms, are like Hansel's stones dropped along the path, though they feel at times more like bread crumbs than stones, each piece eaten up by time's passing. Once in a while, Mr. Leopold sits in a kitchen chair by the sliding glass door, breathes, follows from stone to stone back to the home of his childhood, aware every step of the way of his heart relaxing and contracting and contracting and contracting.

BIG CAT

It's a Thursday in winter, and Louise is growing increasingly convinced that her husband is in love with their cat. Though he has a bad hip and can barely walk without grimacing, she has noticed that he, her husband (not the cat, who is also a he), often gets down on all fours to play or talk or sometimes caress the cat because, he says, "the cat likes to interact best when one is down at his level."

This morning, Louise's husband rises first. She usually wakes him, but today he gets up when the cat comes and lies down on his chest, purring loudly. Louise remains in bed, upstairs, while the two, her husband and the cat, go down to the kitchen. From what she used to consider the comfort of her bed and now is not so sure about, Louise can hear her husband, down in the kitchen, talking to the cat. He is using words he used to use in his interactions with her, terms of endearment like Bubbe, or the shortened, Bubs. "I love you, Bubs," she can hear him say. It's possible, Louise thinks, that her husband is merely lazy in his use of language and hasn't come up with a separate endearment for the cat. In fact, she tries to comfort herself with that explanation. But upon reflection, she realizes that he no longer calls her Bubs. That perhaps he hasn't for quite a few days.

Now, the sky is still dark and her husband and the cat are alone in the dark kitchen. Yes, dark. Because Louise's husband never turns on a light when he doesn't have to. He prefers to operate by what leaks from the refrigerator or the microwave, or what scraps of moonlight or predawn twilight make their way in through the windows.

The cat is male and moody and handsome and seems to grow larger by the day. Louise's husband insists that he isn't fat, just large, and Louise is inclined to agree with him. But for how many years can a cat continue growing?

Louise sits in bed and gives herself over to considering the matter. She suspects that the house may be under the kind of spell one sees depicted in cheap horror films, whereby the cat grows larger and larger on love, and, because her husband has transferred his love from her to the cat, Louise is shrinking as the cat grows. In equal measure. Before this, she hadn't thought that love was a supply with limits, but now she can see that it is, at least where it concerns her husband.

She knows that confessing to anyone her idea about the conservation of size in their house and its relation to the flow of her husband's love will make her seem ridiculous or crazy, so she decides to keep her thoughts to herself. Still, she determines that she will begin to mark her height on a wall in the spare room. And to weigh herself regularly, recording the measurements in her diary. In a parallel column she will record as best she can the changes in the cat's size, though his length will be difficult to measure, as a cat's length often is.

BIG ROUND THING

A woman finds herself stuck on the surface of her skin. As on the shoulder of a highway at night in the rain. Or the roof of an apartment building in the city in summer afternoon sun and accumulated heat. Maybe a dirty kitchen floor, beside a pile of ants and a sticky patch of spilled orange juice. Her entire consciousness sits there, on the surface, like hairs only without the follicles. She's shut out of the main living quarters of her being. Never mind anything in the basement or deeper recesses.

So she sits outside her house, on her deck, under a bunch of oak trees whose tops toss about wildly in the summer wind. She lets her hair grow. She lets it blow around like the tree tops. Doing this, she begins to feel that she's getting somewhere. Unkempt hair feels like a start. If you let go, your body will tell you things, she hears a voice say.

She sees a woman planting something round and large in the corner of a field. Like a large cabbage. Or a melon. Or an unidentified object from outer space. Or the seed of a tree big enough to split open a life. Or a dream plant, the kind that sprouts wild dogs and octopi. Or French horns and cornucopias. The planting isn't happening in the world outside. There isn't a field beyond the trees beyond her deck. She sees the planting but she doesn't see it. The planting is nowhere but also right with her. It has to be done alone, on one's own, the voice says.

Go find the big round thing, the voice says.

THANK YOU LETTER

I heard on the radio yesterday that scientists conducted an experiment recently on a variety of desert ants and found that they have some kind of internal pedometer that measures distance to food sources, and it is this system of measurement along with a kind of celestial navigation that helps them get where they need to go. In the experiment some ants were given leg extensions, like stilts, while others had part of their legs amputated, and those with longer legs marched past their destination while the amputees stopped far short of the same goal. Articles about this phenomenon don't spend much time on the cruelty of amputation or on how miraculous it is that the amputees continued to march at all. Anyway, remember that book you recommended to me 19 years ago? Well I'm finally reading it. Yeah, just yesterday I remembered how all those years ago you were visiting and we were all sitting at the dining room table eating baked ziti, one of my husband's specialties that year, crispy on top, with fresh tomatoes, abundant garlic, all that ricotta and mozzarella and fresh herbs, and you mentioned, your throat moving inside your neck, still showing signs of having just swallowed a bite, that I ought to check out a book of stories you had read recently. Scanning my memory files, I realize that may be the last time we actually *had* a conversation and it wasn't *much* of a conversation, but it was enough to make me desire you at the time since books are my primary love and anyone who recommends one that I might appreciate and does so with their neck exposed the way yours was, right there, so out in the open it could have been blasting out trumpet sounds only it was pretty quiet, your neck, but rough and a little red from shaving, and so tangible, so begging to be touched, or scratched, is likely to elicit longing in me. Yes, that's it, I longed for just a second to scratch your neck but not angrily, erotically I think, though it's also true I may be making all of this up since all I really remember from that dinner was the ziti and the bricks behind you, the way the bricks from the fireplace made a dark backdrop that began to swallow your outline so you seemed to dissipate before my very eyes, or maybe not dissipate but grow more distant or less detailed, more a part of something larger and less clearly yourself. More importantly I suppose, I watched your words travel across towards me, leaving your lips to set out on their journey through the air between us and they came out in a perfect line, those words of yours. Each word was broken into its component letters, and each letter was like an ant marching across the table to me, only they didn't march across the actual table, they marched in the air above the table. Not only did they march across the air to me, but that line of ants mentioning a book I might like to read have continued marching for 19 years, making circles around me, sometimes veering off for months or even years at a time, heading to an anthill or library or wherever there are bits of bread or bagel about, under the counter or near the trash can, sometimes under the stove, where that drawer comes out and it's tough to get the broom or vacuum, or maybe they've been finding far off cream of wheat grains since once I heard you could lead ants away that way, and then, after their long march-about, they came back yesterday of all days, and one little ant step at a time they marched right into my right ear and into my brain and drove me so crazy I had to hop in the car and go straight to the library to relieve the itchy tickling feeling those darned ant words were making in my brain after all this time, and it's a good thing too and that's why I'm writing to you to tell you, thanks, I like it, I like it a lot. It's a good book.

THE LOVER

Lying on her sofa under a sage-green afghan knit for her by her mother, she thinks about how, since it is Monday, most people are at work. This is a kind of work, she tells herself, meaning reading, even if she isn't paid to do it. She's reading a story in which a woman is lying in bed next to her lover, and this causes her, the woman reading, to wonder what it would feel like to be lying in bed next to her own lover. The woman in the story doesn't seem to be in love with her lover since, as the story progresses, it becomes apparent that she is still in love with her former lover, though she reveals this to the reader but not to her lover. The woman in the story's lover is therefore not necessarily the one she most loves but the one she is involved with sexually and this use of the word leads her, the woman reading the story, to look up the word *lover* in the dictionary. She really doesn't want to get up from the sofa to get the dictionary, but fortunately, there's one close by, a fat red dictionary on the carpet under the coffee table next to where she's lying, not far from the fire, reading, and if she holds onto the sofa with the bottom half of her body, inserting her left foot between the couch cushions to anchor her, she can stretch her torso and her arm far enough to reach the dictionary without actually getting up from the sofa. Once she manages to do this and then re-situates herself comfortably under her afghan, she looks up the word *lover* and finds that the first definition is a person who loves. She's pretty sure that her husband, who loves lots of things – Miles Davis and Proust and Cheetos and football and charcoal drawings and the landscapes of Egon Schiele and walking at dawn and coffee and their cat – loves her. And she, like him, loves many things, including him. So they are, she reasons, lovers. Still, one doesn't frequently refer to one's husband as one's lover, and indeed, were she to talk with her sister on the phone and were her sister to say, what have you been up to and were she to respond, oh, I spent the day lying in bed having coffee with my lover, she's willing to bet her sister would feel a little envious, more envious than she might were she to say to her sister that she spent the day lying in bed drinking coffee with her husband. She decides she is going to begin calling him her lover, referring to him in her mind as her lover, and she believes that by doing so, she will more and more deeply come to think of him as her lover and will therefore be more likely to write her own story about lying in bed with her lover, just like the woman in the story she is reading. And this would be pleasing since she likes the woman in the story, and also she would like to write her own story. She sympathizes with the woman in the story. When the woman's lover asks her about a former lover – the woman's lover wants to know about the other lover, about how the love affair ended – the woman finds that though she wouldn't mind telling about it, she can't because she starts to tear up when she thinks about it, though she isn't sure why, and even though she knows the love affair is over, being asked about it makes her realize she hasn't entirely taken in the concept of over. So the woman in the story turns away from her lover, letting the light coming in through the blind hit the side of her face. If she, the woman reading, were lying in bed with her husband lover and were asked about her former lover, she thinks she would come to more deeply understand the woman in the story who begins to recall a mysterious letter she received from her former lover. The woman in the story has read and reread the letter many times, examining it for clues, trying to understand the impulse behind its writing, but the letter contains only a snippet from a poem written by someone else. It feels to the woman in the story as if the letter makes any sense of closure impossible. The letter is like a hole into dark space. The woman in the story looks and looks and looks and there is still only darkness, which is sometimes the case at the end of things with a lover even if there isn't a mysterious letter to ponder. The woman reading the story has often wished that her final communication with her own last lover had been more satisfying, but the more she tries to recreate their last conversation in her mind, the more she tries to see what the sky looked like, whether it was dark and cloudy, which might have been significant, or a bright blue sky with puffy clouds and sunlight streaming down like in religious paintings, the more blurry and unsatisfying the whole interaction becomes. So, she thinks, if she, like the woman in the story she is reading, finds herself lying in bed with her lover and he asks her to tell him about her former lover, she decides that, like the woman in the story, she will probably refrain from doing so. She might even get up and go to use the bathroom and when she returns, change the conversation to something she's just learned about how Proust wrote under seven woolen blankets, wearing a fur coat, with three hot-water bottles and a lighted fire, while outside, in the streets of Paris, people fell ill from the heat. She thinks that, since her lover seems to her to enjoy a high degree of discomfort in his own creative practices, he will appreciate this and the added fact that Proust wrote page after page in an awkward and strained position, with a leaky penholder and an ink pot almost always empty. She notices that, already, in thinking through the problem of how to get out of talking with her lover about her former lover, she has begun to think of her husband more and more frequently as her lover, and she is beginning to feel an exciting alteration in her already deep fondness for him. She thinks maybe she will ask him to join her for a walk later, and while they walk, she may reach out and hold his hand. If they stop to look for the kingfisher, where it often stands on a post, she will lean over and kiss him, and when she returns she will write a letter to her friend in Virginia, beginning the letter by saying, it is Monday afternoon, and I just got back from a walk with my lover.

THE PROBLEM

Here is a woman. This woman is taking a train to another city.

Another woman is supposed to meet her there, in that other city, at the train station.

She has told that other woman, whom she has never met before, that she will be wearing a read coat and a read hat.

She told the woman this so that she would be able to recognize her in a crowd of strangers.

But she said this on the telephone instead of writing it in a letter or other message so she is concerned that the woman who is coming to meet her will be looking for a woman in a red coat and red hat.

Actually, her coat and hat have a story written on them.

The story begins at the top of her hat and continues moving down the page of her hat and coat from left to right but in a slight downward spiral so that the reader can either read by circling the woman wearing the read hat and coat or the woman can spin slowly in place so as to facilitate the reader's reading of the story.

In fact, she has done this little spinning dance several times in the last few months, ever since she was given the hat and coat from a writer friend who also happens to design clothing.

The story on the hat and coat is about a man named George who dreams he has lost all his teeth. He can see them in the bottom of a pool and stands at poolside for quite some time in the story, strategizing a plan for retrieving his teeth.

Although George does come up with a plan and collects all his teeth, there is of course no way the dream dentist can return the teeth successfully to George's gums.

Fortunately, George wakes up in the story to the sound of a tea kettle and discovers that he is still in possession of his teeth though he has been thrust into a rather larger psychic crisis, which is not resolved in the story.

Many people in the woman's family and in her local community have read the story.

In fact, she has become a minor celebrity in her town where she is a favorite at art centers and coffee shops, and other places where people are interested in reading hats and coats.

But on the phone, earlier, when she spoke to the woman who is supposed to be meeting her, all she had said was that she'd be wearing a read hat and coat and she now realizes there is no way to explain that silent "a" to the woman who is, presumably, wandering the crowd, searching for her.

OSMOSIS

When we first started practicing yoga together, my husband had difficulty focusing. He'd reach over from his purple mat and grab my arm affectionately during Cat Chaturanga or poke me in the shoulder during Blown Palm, or he'd leap off his mat to go spit in the sink during Warrior pose. And in the midst of the peacefulness of Corpse pose he'd laugh and impersonate people from his past like some guy I never met who played Doc in his high school's production of *West Side Story* or famous people with distinct styles of speech like Sean Connery. Throughout his antics, I remained very focused, and even when he tickled me, I maintained my posture and breathing. Now, several months into our practice, my husband breathes deeply and steadily and listens attentively to the instructor's commands and commentary. He says not a word and never budges from his mat whereas I have begun to impersonate the instructor, kiss my husband on the neck during Mountain pose and jump up to check my cellphone during Corpse pose. His inattention seems to have passed into me through the invisible though permeable membrane that is all that separates us after so many years of marriage.

Rilke, 2017, at Shaw's

I'm standing at the egg department at the grocery
store. I hear chickens under the sound of the
refrigerators. My feet begin to sweat. It is important to
pay attention to glandular involvement. I have to change
my life.

Roy Rogers, Where Are You?

When you said, over coffee the other day, that my canceling our lunch date the previous Friday had been a trigger for you, I take it you were not referring to Roy Rogers's horse. Had you been, I think you might have been suggesting that my not being able to meet was like a faithful horse. You would've meant that it was like a co-star in the movie of your life, or something like that. You might've meant that our lunch would have been like something you might ride away on into a sunset or a silver screen, or that together we might make people laugh and sick children smile.

The word *trigger*, however, as I believe you meant it, is, in my opinion, much overused these days. Allow me to explain. Trigger, in the psychological literature, and in the therapeutic milieu, usually refers to those suffering from PTSD, and though you've been deeply disappointed in my behavior towards you over the years, as you have explained to me extensively and with admirable devotion and frequency over those many years, that disappointment hardly qualifies as trauma. I can't help wondering if Roy was ever disappointed in his horse, or more probably, if Trigger was ever disappointed in Roy. Or, perhaps, if Trigger was traumatized by Roy or some trainer hired by Roy to prepare Trigger for the screen life. Was Roy ever traumatized by being thrown, even inadvertently, from Trigger during a ride or rehearsal? And if so, how did Trigger, or Roy, behave in the aftermath of such a situation? Trigger, it turns out, was a palomino stallion, and remained a stallion his whole life, which itself might have been traumatic for him. He was never bred and has no descendants. Do horses concern themselves with continuing their line?

I'm not fond of the word *trigger,* especially as regards people and their reactions and overreactions. The word, as you used it, connotes violence, and seems deeply though not always consciously linked to our overly violent gun culture (a culture about which I've heard you express loud and public disapproval) but it also (the word) is often used in an attempt to suggest that those who are triggered have no power or control, no responsibility, for their own reactions/misbehavior. A couple thousand years of philosophy and spiritual writing offers, I believe, ample wisdom to counter this viewpoint, suggesting that rather than resign ourselves to our own behaviors being the uncontrollable result of other people's treatment of us, we have the power to cultivate the discipline that enables us to refrain from such reactivity.

When Roy put a kilt on Trigger for an appearance

in Glasgow, might his horse have felt Roy was taking things too far? Might he have wanted to lash out? Or when he had to climb three or four flights of stairs to visit sick children, might he have looked at Roy with a look that said he'd had enough and walked out for good, with no goodbye, after a many years relationship?

Since we no longer speak, as you felt *triggered* (as you explained to me that day in the coffee shop) into shooting me dead from your life (picking up your things and walking away without saying goodbye and refusing to answer my phone calls) I am writing to request, on behalf of all those people in your present and future, *with* whom I have no intercourse but *for* whom I feel compassion, that you consider a more mindful use of language. And here I get confused. Roy thought he was making a good choice in calling Trigger Trigger, since he thought it expressed something about Trigger's quick wit, for Trigger could do all sorts of tricks such as sit in a chair and sign his name X with a pencil, but when he took away Trigger's original name, Golden Cloud, was he robbing him of an identity, a connection to something of nature and therefore more true to a horse? What, indeed, is in a name? I know that mindfulness itself is a bit of an overused term in our present day and age, though, to my thinking, the peripheral effects, the connotations, and the collateral damages of mindfulness are preferable to the overuse of other locutions and metaphors used without conscious forethought.

In the end, Trigger died at the age of 31, which is old for a horse. You ended our relationship after twenty-five years, which is old for some relationships but not others. Roy had Trigger stuffed, though the language he used was probably something like *preserved*. His hide, Trigger's, was stretched over a foam likeness of himself and then put on display in the Roy Rogers and Dale Evans Museum in Apple Valley. I don't know of any taxidermists who stuff abstractions such as friendships, though I am interested in what the concrete expression of ours would look like and what fabric they would stretch to cover that shape. Though maybe I have got it all wrong and you didn't actually kill our relationship but symbolically killed me dead from your life so that what would be taxidermied (is that a verb?) would be me. I know what I look like. And I am pretty sure I know of someone who could easily build a foam likeness of me. It turns out Trigger's taxidermied remains sold for $266,500 at auction. I'm not sure of the implications of that.

I'd be willing to bet that Roy and Trigger loved each other, despite any disagreements or lashings out that occurred over the years. Ditto you and me. For now, I enjoy imagining the shape of our long-lived though now dead relationship and wonder what price it might command, wherever they auction such things.

BORROWED TRANSITIONS

As unexpected as it seems, the cat fell asleep on its perch and I continued to read about somatic stimuli as sources for dreams. I like old academic citations. And received a message from a woman asking me to go seek owls on a beach with her.

And another wanting to share annoyances and coffee. *That* woman fell out of her pants. I mean she forgot how to dance. I mean money changes the way a person holds her hands, and often how she stands, while she speaks. "A faucet, once replaced, is nothing to worry about," she said, and adjusted her scarf.

"True," I answered. I can assert my will in matters of practice though not in matters of content and have been looking for a published discussion of this phenomenon.

When she left, she took the light with her, which seemed appropriate, it being winter.

Eventually, that thing we sometimes call erotic did return. It comes back after a long hiatus like failed operations in that old game of that name, when you try to remove the ulna and your tweezers hit the sensor. I mean a light or buzz goes off here and there in the body. In the arm, the rib cage, the knee, behind the eyes.

I never thought the postal service would succumb but look at the look of things.

Happily, in the pit out back, coyotes can be heard howling in packs which is refreshing if you consider it from the right perspective.

And isn't reading books from other centuries so much more satisfying and conducive to the creation of interesting energies in one's immediate environs? I mean, its impact on the sofa seems ample evidence.

Curbside in Barnstable, I ran into a painter with red and yellow and orange smeared all over his pants. "Why are your hands always so Célan?" I asked. I sometimes suffer from dyslexic speech patterns but rarely correct my mistakes. Also, I'm not so wrinkled up all the time but I squint when I forget my eyeglasses.

He didn't answer me. He was chewing earlier remarks I'd made, drawing on Freud and Michelangelo and some contemporary critic whose name I can't recall. "Can't You See I'm Burning?" the article had been titled.

"Hey," I said, "you know how much I admire your work, right?"

I offered him coffee in a paper cup, and sugar in little packets just in case. I tend to plan ahead. I also know how to talk sometimes though I have a distaste for topical humor.

Spider

When I asked E, she told me, through the small
cloudy screen of the confessional in St. Joseph's Church,
the only place she'd agree to be interviewed and which
we had to sneak into midday on a Tuesday when neither
the priest nor any attentive parishioners were around to
notice two women, neither dressed in priest's garb – no
alb, no cassock, not even a detachable clerical collar –
entering the two doors of the confessional, not of course
for confession, that she liked to converse in the dark
intimacy of that space since it created conditions akin to
lyric poetry, where she, the one being interviewed, could
speak, responding to my questions, but at the same time
she could be alone with her thoughts, talking aloud as if
to herself in that privacy offered by the screen and the
dark and history of that space and all the secrets and sins
that had been unburdened there, and of course she knew
I would be there listening, not receiving what she said as
confession but attentively receiving what that privacy
enabled her to pull up from places deep within, from the
cells and memories, the closets and cupboards in her,

from the dresser drawers, the crawl spaces, the attics and cottages and caves, from the rocks and stones and trees in her, and it's possible that to do so she needed that separated space, that screen between us, so that she might reveal parts of her physical self or conduct some physical contortions that she might feel too self conscious to perform in front of me but that were necessary in order for her to discuss the matter which I had asked her to permit me an interview about, and that was, of course, as anyone who has read her work might suspect, the hole that ran through her core, a hole she'd described as starting out small – really just a pinprick through which she'd initially felt cool air pass, and a little later had seen light travel through when she'd gone to a dark space with a flashlight to test what she sensed to be true but had had difficulty believing – but which had grown over the course of a few brief months to become a tunnel with a diameter about the size of a grapefruit only shaped, she had come to realize much later, like a scarab, that symbol in ancient Egypt of the soul and which she had inadvertently created – the shape, not her soul – through her core by meditation and, she said she needed to be very clear about this, not very intense or informed meditation, a meditation style and practice, rather, that she'd somewhat fumbled her way into, but once the hole had developed, the scarab-shaped hole in her core the outlines of which, while she spoke with me in the privacy of the confessional, she could touch with the soft tips of her fingers, most of the time she kept covered by t-shirt or sweater or jacket in colder weather, but through which, even covered, she could feel things pass and because of the condition of being so porous, she had found it necessary to go out often at night, among the sounds of frogs, crickets, owls, drenched in the light of the full moon or wrapped in moonless dark, torso exposed, so that the things of the world could more easily pass through her, things both physical and metaphysical, and in fact, she added, it was only after the development of the scarab that she'd even thought to enter a church of any kind, that the space of a confessional had developed any appeal for her, but since the scarab, she'd often felt drawn to such spaces, not only confessionals which, she chuckled while saying, she confessed had become among her favorite spaces, but also apses, choir lofts, sabhas and stupas, wats, pagodas, mosques, Gurdwaras, shuls, and basilicas, and other places holy and sacred, crypts, tombs, cemeteries, shrines, and while in such spaces she felt, she explained, an intensification in the vibration of the energy that was at all times like a current passing through her, a current whose density and hue and pitch, she said, varied immensely from place to place and also of course depending on her state, on whether she were meditating or not, on how attentive she was being at any given moment to her own breath and how hospitable she made herself to love, yes, that was the phrase she used, how hospitable to love, and I didn't want to interrupt her as she spoke since it seemed the more quiet I became, there, on my side of the confessional screen, and so unlike what I imagined a priest to be but then thinking maybe not,

maybe I was doing precisely what priests did, making
myself as present and attentive and unobtrusive as
possible, the more likely it was that she could reach into
her own dark cavities and pull out both pains and
illuminations and, offering them up, lighten her internal
weight, and through the intensity of my (or in some
situations, the priest's) listening, I (or a priest) could
keep that process going, sustain it for longer perhaps
than she (or some penitent) might manage to sustain it
without such a witness, and so, despite the questions I
might have asked, I kept as quiet as I could, the only
sounds my breath and the occasional creak the seat made
as I shifted my weight, and, when I felt it appropriate, a
humming of barely audible assent, and let her continue
speaking in this interview which I have to admit wasn't
really an interview in the usual sense at all except that,
also, I had the sense as I sat there breathing in the dark,
that she would, if I were patient, answer all the questions
I'd prepared even without my voicing them since there
was, I believed, in her process, on the other side of the
screen, something terrifically receptive, at frequencies far
beneath speech, so that she seemed to know those
questions without needing any prompting from me, and
I sensed, further, passing back and forth in the dark air
between us, a trust, one bestowed by this space and its
history (despite the innumerable betrayals that must also
have happened there) and the current flowing through
her, and as I sensed this trust I knew also that she'd
removed her shirt on her side of the confessional, that
the scarab had to be absolutely unfettered for such

communication, and that, though how I should know this I can't say, as she spoke, in addition to all else that channeled through her, a tiny spider was, while she spoke and I listened, making its way through that passage in her, for what reason I couldn't be certain, a tiny spider that had taken up residence in the not often used confessional, had spun its web in some corner there and now had lowered itself and was carrying itself through her, in the absolute silence in which spiders move.

LAMP

We have taken to walking through unfamiliar neighborhoods during these winter evenings. We walk in the evening not so that we may press our faces to the glass of strange houses and spy on the inhabitants, nor because we like to see garish displays of holiday lights (though we do enjoy those), but because, in some houses, we catch sight of single lamps and their elegant, glowing skirt-like light. We find the lamps comforting, especially if they are floor lamps and there's a chair near the lamp, or a bookcase in view, beside or behind the chair. The lamps are in full possession of their soundlessness; their light lacks clumsiness or aggression. They don't flicker. They don't attempt to fill entire spaces, don't pour over all the furniture like a swimming pool turned upside down, don't, like TVs, rage one moment and collapse the next, filling rooms with the herky-jerky light of plot and action and crime drama. They almost seem to practice silent prayer, to have cultivated the stillness of yogis, these lone lamps. And we are looking to them to solve a design issue that has recently arisen in our home. For recently, we moved a lamp, a mid-century modern floor lamp, from one room, the kitchen, to another, the living room, and while we are very pleased with the lamp in its new spot, we are experiencing a thunderous absence in the space where the lamp formerly stood. We have been searching in home stores, in consignment shops, in online marketplaces, but thus far nothing has called out to us. Meanwhile, with each day that passes, the space where the lamp no longer stands in the kitchen grows louder and louder; it's downright deafening in the dark of early morning, when we tend to sit in silence at the kitchen table and sip coffee and read or write. When the lamp was there, its light filled only that corner, and the kitchen felt quiet and calm, the surrounding darkness cocoon-like and fertile. The lamp cast a mellow light, a light one might be tempted to associate with Chet Baker played softly through a speaker in the next room, but even that would be inaccurate since the mellow light was absolutely silent, more like the warmth and joy and love Antonio Machado described in his poem of sleeping and dreams and the marvelous error of discovering springs and bees and suns inside his heart. Evenings, we rarely turned on the lamp when it stood in the kitchen, but its presence bespoke security, solidity. It said to us that if ever age robbed us of the ability to eat our lentils by the sometimes steady and other times flickering light of the candles we so regularly depend on at dinner, it, the lamp, would be there for us, at the ready, stalwart, a mighty friend. We have discussed moving the lamp back, of restoring the old order and peace to our home, but we agree that it seems so happy in the living room, by the reading chair, where it gets more use and, though it never complained in its former location, one can see that in its new spot it is less crowded. And so we walk, and look into the homes of strangers, believing a solution will present itself, and at the same time training ourselves to grow more and more comfortable with the dark, which is after all where we all must reside eventually.

Bio

Mary Kane is the author of *On Tuesday, Elizabeth* (Little Dipper, 2020), *Door* (One Bird Books, 2015) and the collaborations *122 Days* with artist Angela Rose (unpublished) and *Luminous* with artist Mark Bilokur (One Bird Books, 2022). She lives, reads, walks, and writes on Cape Cod.

Great Big Thanks

I am deeply grateful to Jill Erickson for reading aloud with me for 20+ years and counting; to Terre McNulty, Stephanie Murphy, Annie Dean, Angela Rose, Barbara Siegel Carlson, Lisa Madsen Rubilar, Rebecca Siegel, Marsha Kroll, Miriam O'Neal, Susan Berlin, Eric Edwards, Judith Benét Richardson, Angela Tanner, Debra Babcock, and Melissa Weidman for your friendship, creativity, insight and ongoing support of my writing for so many years; to Elizabeth McHale, Stephanie Madsen-Pixler and Christopher Madsen, strangers who generously read this manuscript for me when I needed the eyes of objective readers; to Lauren Wolk and Peter Orner for being kind enough to read the manuscript; to Jim Morgan for his friendship and for making this book possible; to Mark Bilokur for the molar; and to Vincent, Lily, and Lionel and all my friends and family.

CPSIA information can be obtained
at www.ICGtesting.com
Printed in the USA
JSHW020032180423
40457JS00001B/32

9 781733 920063